Straight Into Danger!

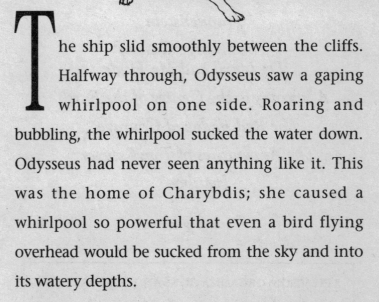

The ship slid smoothly between the cliffs. Halfway through, Odysseus saw a gaping whirlpool on one side. Roaring and bubbling, the whirlpool sucked the water down. Odysseus had never seen anything like it. This was the home of Charybdis; she caused a whirlpool so powerful that even a bird flying overhead would be sucked from the sky and into its watery depths.

The ship began to spin toward the deadly pool. "Turn to starboard!" Odysseus roared at his crew. "Turn toward the opposite cliff!"

Wishbone Classics

THE ODYSSEY

by Homer

retold by Joanne Mattern

Interior illustrations by Hokanson/Cichetti
Wishbone illustrations by Kathryn Yingling

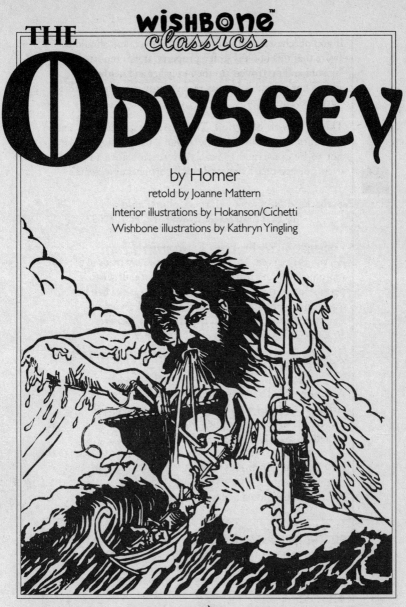

HarperPaperbacks

A Division of HarperCollinsPublishers

This is a work of fiction. The characters, incidents, and dialogues are products of the author's imagination and are not to be construed as real. Any resemblance to actual events or persons, living or dead, is entirely coincidental.

HarperPaperbacks *A Division of* HarperCollins*Publishers*
10 East 53rd Street, New York, N.Y. 10022

Copyright ©1996 Big Feats! Entertainment

Cover photographs by Carol Kaelson

A Creative Media Applications Production
Art Direction by Fabia Wargin Design
Project Management by Ellen Weiss
Edited by Matt Levine

First printing: April 1996

Printed in the United States of America

HarperPaperbacks and colophon are trademarks of
HarperCollins*Publishers*
WISHBONE is a trademark and service mark of
Big Feats! Entertainment

❖ 10 9 8

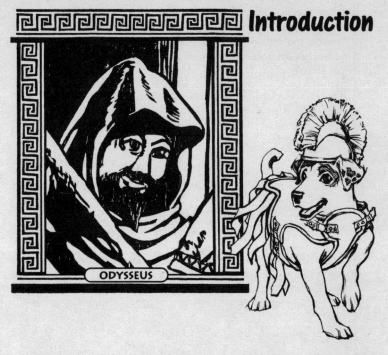

ODYSSEUS

All set to enter a world of action, adventure, drama, and laughs? Then come along with me, **Wishbone**. You may have seen me on my TV show. Often I am the main character and sometimes I am the sidekick, but I'm always right in the middle of a thrilling story. Now, I'm going to be your guide as we explore one of the world's greatest books — THE ODYSSEY. Together we'll meet a lot of interesting characters and discover places we've never been! I guarantee lots of surprises too! So find a nice comfy chair, and get ready to read with **Wishbone.**

Table of Contents

Homer

Homer was the ancient Greek poet who told the story of THE ODYSSEY. At least, that's what most people think. It's hard to say for sure, because scholars (the people who study a subject in great detail) believe that THE ODYSSEY was composed between 800 and 700 B.C. That is a long—LONG—time ago, especially if you're talking dog years.

Tradition says that Homer lived either on the eastern shore of the Aegean Sea or on the Greek island of Khios. Tradition also says that Homer was blind, but that never stopped him from being a great poet. You see, in those days, the Greeks didn't have a written language. What they did have was oration—that is, the Greeks told stories out loud to audiences instead of writing them down. *The Odyssey* is called oral poetry, and Homer recited the whole story from memory!

By filling his tale with repetition and colorful images, Homer was able to remember the whole story of *The Odyssey* each time he told it. Also, he probably added or changed small details in the story to keep it interesting. **Clever guy.**

Homer is famous for another story, an epic poem called *The Iliad*. *The Iliad* tells about the famous Trojan War. The Trojan War was a pretty big deal in Homer's time and was the reason Odysseus left home in the first place.

ABOUT THE ODYSSEY

The Odyssey begins on an ancient Greek island called Ithaca. In those days, the Greeks believed that powerful gods and goddesses affected everyday life. In fact, there was a separate god or goddess for almost everything in the world.

Zeus was the king of all the gods. He caused thunderstorms and hurled lightning bolts through the sky. Other important gods were Poseidon, the god of the oceans, Hermes, the messenger god, and Athena, the goddess of wisdom. All the gods lived on top of a huge mountain called Olympus.

Although there are many gods in *The*

Odyssey, the hero of this tale is a man named Odysseus. (*The Odyssey* gets its name from Odysseus.) Odysseus was the king of Ithaca.

Odysseus fought in the Trojan War with another Greek king, Menelaus. Together they fought against the people of Troy for ten years! Odysseus had left his wife, Penelope, and his baby son, Telemachus, behind in Ithaca. While he was fighting the war, he missed them very much.

Finally, the war was over and the Greeks had won. Menelaus and Odysseus set out for home. In time, Menelaus reached his home, but for Odysseus, getting home proved to be even more difficult than the war itself. Odysseus's long, exciting journey is exactly what *The Odyssey* is all about.

MAIN CHARACTERS

Antinous (an-TIN-oh-us)—leader of the suitors
Eurylochus (you-RILL-oh-kus)—a member of
   Odysseus's crew
Menelaus (men-ah-LAY-us)—king of Sparta
Odysseus (oh-DISS-ee-us)—king of Ithaca
Penelope (pen-ELL-oh-pee)—Odysseus's wife
Telemachus (te-LE-mah-kus)—Odysseus's son

Gods and Goddesses

The Greeks and Romans worshipped many of the same gods and goddesses, but referred to them by different names.

GREEK NAME	ROMAN NAME
Athena (ah-THEE-nah) —goddess of wisdom	**Minerva** (mih-NER-vah)
Hermes (HER-meez) —messenger god	**Mercury** (MER-kyoor-ee)
Poseidon (poh-SY-don) —god of the sea	**Neptune** (NEP-toon)
Zeus (ZOOS) —king of the gods	**Jupiter** (JOO-pit-er)

SETTING

Important Places

Aeaea (ay-EE-uh)—island ruled by Circe

Hades (HAY-deez)—the Land of the Dead

Ithaca (ITH-ah-kah)—Greek island ruled by Odysseus

Mount Olympus (oh-LIM-puss)—home of the gods

Ogygia (oh-JIJ-jee-ah)—home of the goddess Calypso

River Styx (STICKS)—the river that leads to Hades

Troy (TROY)—city in Asia where the Trojan War was fought

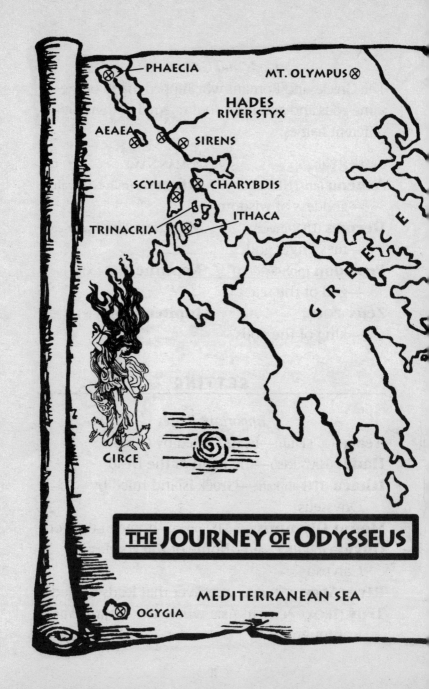

PHAECIA

MT. OLYMPUS ⊗

HADES
RIVER STYX

AEAEA ⊗   ⊗ SIRENS

SCYLLA   ⊗ CHARYBDIS

TRINACRIA   ITHACA

G
R
E
E
C
E

CIRCE

THE JOURNEY OF ODYSSEUS

MEDITERRANEAN SEA

⊗ OGYGIA

TROY ⊗

TURKEY

AEGEAN SEA

LOTUS
EATERS ⊗

CRETE

CAVE OF THE CYCLOPS ⊗

1
A Hero Far Away

Pardon me, did you see a cat run by? A little gray thing? Furry? Beady eyes? You didn't? Hmmm. Where could he have gone?

Now don't get the idea that I'm not fast enough to catch a cat. It's just that today I don't feel like catching a cat.

How far did I chase that furball anyway? I must have run a good twenty blocks! Whoa! I'd better head home.

Wait a minute. This is starting to remind me of a book I know about another guy who traveled far from home and then had a really rough time getting back. The story is called THE ODYSSEY, and it was first told almost three thousand years ago by a man named Homer.

The story begins on the Greek island of Ithaca (ITH-ah-kah), where Queen Penelope (pen-ELL-oh-pee) is waiting for her husband, Odysseus (oh-DISS-ee-us), to come home....

Queen Penelope sat weeping in her chamber. Twenty years ago, her husband, King Odysseus, had gone away to war, and he hadn't yet returned. He might have perished in a battle, his body long since turned to dust. Or he might have died at sea.

Queen Penelope refused to believe any of this. In her heart her husband was alive. Somewhere in the wide world the mighty King Odysseus was alive and would come home to her.

The Queen stood up and began to pace her royal chamber. She gazed upon the stone walls, brightly painted with many colors. She felt the soft red carpeting beneath her feet. She smelled the sweet perfumes and scented oils that wafted through the air, and watched as the light from torches and candles danced upon her endless piles of gold jewelry. But none of these things could cheer her heart or make her smile.

A knock came upon her chamber door. Penelope wiped away a tear and tossed her golden hair back from her ivory shoulders. She opened the door and was greeted by her son, Telemachus (te-LE-mah-kus).

Telemachus had been just a baby when his father went away to war. Now he was a fine tall man with black curly hair and a sad smile that was very much like his father's.

"Why do you cry, Mother?" Telemachus asked.

"I was thinking of your father," Penelope said.

His eyes met hers, and for a moment both were silent. "The suitors are requesting an appearance," Telemachus said at last. **A suitor is a man who wants to marry someone. These particular suitors are disgusting, as you'll soon see. These men have pestered Penelope to marry one of them. And they aren't asking politely! They demand that Penelope choose one man from among them, and meanwhile, they make her life miserable. They are a very low-down pack of hounds.**

Penelope detested the suitors. For three long years, all the wealthy men of Ithaca had wanted to marry Penelope. She told them over and over again that her husband was alive, but no one believed her. The suitors insisted that it was time for Penelope to choose a new husband—a man who would become King of Ithaca.

To make things even worse, the suitors were a wicked bunch of men. Hundreds of them burst into her house every day, screaming and shouting and singing disgusting songs. They gambled and swore, broke her furniture, and ate her food. Finally, after they'd had their fill, the suitors would fall down asleep right in her house.

Penelope hated all of them. She prayed to Zeus (ZOOS), king of all the gods, to bring her true husband home again. She dreamed of the day when King Odysseus would return from war and deliver a just punishment to the many suitors. Sadly, this day seemed very far away.

Penelope had done everything she could to stop the suitors from forcing her to marry one of them. She even tried to trick them. One day

A funeral shroud is a cloth wrapped around a body before it is buried.

Penelope announced that she would choose a husband as soon as she finished weaving a funeral shroud for Odysseus's dying father, Laertes (lay-UR-teez). Every day Penelope sat at her loom, weaving the shroud. But every night, while the suitors slept, she crept to her loom and unraveled all the work she had done.

Penelope worked on Laertes' shroud for a long time, but eventually the suitors guessed what she was up to. When Penelope's trick was revealed, the suitors became more demanding than ever.

"Tell the suitors I shall not appear," Penelope said to her son.

"Mother, you must. They are angry, and they will stop at nothing to see you."

"I shall not marry while my husband is alive," Penelope said firmly.

"Mother," said Telemachus, taking her by the hand, "it is only a matter of time before my father comes home. When he does, he will make these suitors sorry for their rudeness. In the meantime, you must go to them and calm their anger."

Penelope stared at the bright blue eyes of her son. He always saw clearly and spoke with reason. With him by her side, she had the strength to face them.

Together, they left her chamber and walked to the staircase that led to the great hall of the house. They stood at the top of the stairs, looking down upon the vast room below.

The suitors were wilder than ever. They gorged themselves on the food. They pounded the tables until the wood split in two, and wrestled, and boxed, and banged their swords.

"Quiet, you fools," a voice echoed in the mighty halls. "Penelope has come!"

The room fell silent. Every eye looked toward the staircase.

Then Antinous (an-TIN-oh-us), the tallest and ugliest of the suitors, stepped forward from the crowd. His hair was thick and greasy, and it stuck to his wide, sweaty face. He was broad and strong, and his hands were twice the size of any other man's.

Penelope detested him the most.

"Penelope!" bellowed Antinous. "It is good that you have come. Tell us which man among us you will choose to marry."

"My husband, the king, is still alive," Penelope said with great dignity. "When he returns, you shall pay for your behavior. Now leave this house and do not return."

Antinous exploded with anger. "That's not

an answer!" he shouted. Then he lifted up a huge chair and hurled it across the room. It crashed into a banquet table and caused it to split. There was a deafening clang of metal trays as plates of breads and meats flew in every direction.

Antinous stepped near Penelope. She stood as straight as she could as he leaned close to her.

"We will stay in your house until you choose a husband," Antinous announced.

Penelope could hide her tears no longer. Weeping bitterly, she ran to her chamber and locked the door.

Telemachus caught Antinous's eyes, and the two men stared at each other.

"What will you say, Telemachus?" sneered Antinous. "You are nothing—nothing but a *little* boy."

Telemachus is more than twenty years old, so why are the suitors calling him a boy? It's because they've known him since he was just a child and don't believe he's grown-up enough to stop them.

Telemachus could not answer. He walked sadly to his mother's room. The two sat together in silence and fear. Below in the mighty hall, the loud noises of the suitors rang through the house.

Telemachus put his arms around his mother and said, "Don't worry, Mother. I know my father will come."

2
Telemachus Takes Action

Poor Telemachus. It's no fun when bigger dogs push you around. Luckily, Telemachus is about to receive some help from someone who is very powerful: the goddess Athena (ah-THEE-nah). She is the goddess of wisdom, and she will give Telemachus some very good advice.

Telemachus was angry when he left his mother's chamber late that night. He hadn't had a good night's rest in a long time, and he knew that he would find no sleep tonight either. The suitors shouted noisily below. Their ugly faces flashed through Telemachus's mind, and their vicious laughter stung his helpless heart.

Telemachus needed to get away from the noise. He crept down the staircase into the hall below. The suitors laughed and danced around him. Telemachus walked through the room as quickly as he could, pretending not to notice them and hoping that they would not notice him. At last he reached the door and slipped outside.

The cold air felt good against his burning face. He breathed deeply as the nighttime sky spread above him. Blazing stars sparkled endlessly in the heavens. The silver moon beamed brightly, shedding soft, gentle light upon the earth below. Telemachus felt overwhelmed.

He leaned against a giant pillar and gazed upon the far horizon. "Will Odysseus really come home someday?" he asked himself aloud. "And if he does, will he be disappointed in me? Shouldn't I rise up against the suitors and protect my home? Shouldn't I defend my mother from Antinous? Shouldn't I—?"

"If King Odysseus is so important to you, why not go and look for him?" called a voice in the darkness.

Startled, Telemachus spun around. "What?" he replied.

"I said, if King Odysseus is so important to you, why not go and look for him?" the voice repeated.

Telemachus stared at the ancient man who appeared before him. It was Mentor, the wisest and most respected elder of the island. His long, thin fingers held a carved wooden staff. His tunic hung loosely from his fragile shoulders, and a fine white beard covered his chin.

"Go and look for him?" replied Telemachus. "Where would I begin? And how did you know I was speaking of my father?"

"I know many things, Telemachus. I can tell you where to begin your search, but you must listen to me and obey carefully."

Telemachus sighed heavily and shook his

head. "Noble Mentor, you have always been a good friend to my family. I have great respect for you. Still, how can I leave my mother by herself?"

"You make excuses well, Telemachus. But that is all they are—excuses!"

Telemachus was silent. Finally Mentor said sarcastically, "Perhaps you are right. Stay here and watch the suitors eat your father's food and treat your mother with disrespect. Soon they shall devour everything. King Odysseus's mighty herds of cattle, pigs, and sheep shall disappear. So will his stores of grain. In time, his wife will be forced to marry. When King Odysseus returns, he will have nothing!"

With that, Mentor turned to leave.

"Mentor, wait!" Telemachus called. The old man turned around and stared at Telemachus. The tension was thick between them. Finally Telemachus spoke.

"All right!" he declared. "I will do it! Tell me where to go, and I shall search for my father."

Mentor smiled as he moved closer to Telemachus. "Tomorrow you must sail to the land of Pylos and ask Nestor if he has any news of your father. He may be able to give you some news. Now go to bed, Telemachus. Tomorrow you have much to do."

Nestor was a great warrior who fought beside Odysseus during the Trojan War.

Nervous and excited, Telemachus obeyed.

When noble Mentor stood alone, a marvelous event took place. A golden light blazed around him. Burning brightly, it grew until it covered the old man completely. When the light finally faded into nothingness, the aged Mentor was gone. In his place stood Athena, goddess of wisdom. She was tall and beautiful, with golden hair that framed her face in silken curls. Athena was the one who, disguised as Mentor, had been speaking with Telemachus. Athena was fond of Odysseus and was determined to do everything in her power to bring him home.

Happy with her work, Athena smiled. Then,

like a whisper on the wind, she flew away to Mount Olympus (oh-LIM-puss), the home of the gods.

Wow! Athena is really something special, isn't she? The gods and goddesses in the old Greek tales often changed into human beings or animals. They were so powerful they could become anyone they wanted. Telemachus is very lucky to have Athena as a friend.

Early the next morning, Telemachus gave orders for a boat to carry him to Pylos. Twenty sailors volunteered to take him. Before the sun was up, Telemachus had started his journey.

"I shall not come home again until I hear news of my father," he vowed.

When Telemachus and his men arrived at Nestor's home in Pylos, they were warmly welcomed. A great feast was held to honor the visitors.

"Thank you for your hospitality,"

Telemachus said to Nestor when the feast was over. "Now I hope you can help me. We know what happened to many of the men who fought during the Trojan War, but we have had no word of the fate of my father, mighty Odysseus. Do you know if he is dead, or if he still lives?"

"My friend, I remember your father well," Nestor replied. "I know that he did not die in battle, and that he left to return to his home on Ithaca. But I don't know what happened to him after that."

Telemachus could not hide his disappointment at Nestor's words. Seeing his sorrow, Nestor had an idea. "Perhaps you should travel to Sparta and visit Menelaus (men-ah-LAY-us)," he suggested. **Odysseus also fought with King Menelaus in the Trojan War. They were great friends.** "He was with Odysseus when I left Troy. Maybe he has more news of your father."

"Thank you, Nestor," Telemachus said. "I will do as you suggest. Perhaps now I can find out what happened to my father."

● ● ● ● ● ●

Telemachus did not get all the answers he needed, so he must continue his journey. Will Menelaus have any news about Odysseus? We'll have to wait and see.

3
A Horrible Discovery

What has Odysseus been doing while Penelope and Telemachus have been suffering at home? Our story is going to jump back ten years in time, to the end of the Trojan War.

When the Trojan War finally ended, King Odysseus was more than ready to head home to Ithaca. He was not only homesick for his native land, he also missed his wife and son terribly. Odysseus didn't think his trip home would be that difficult. Instead the journey turned out to be so long and dangerous that nowadays, when we speak about a long, hard journey, we call it an "odyssey." Odyssey...Odysseus. Get it?

Now let's catch up with Odysseus at the start of his journey....

King Odysseus stood on the sandy, sun-baked shore of Troy. He was a tall man, and his shoulders, arms, and legs bulged with muscles. Long black hair streamed around his handsome face. Odysseus was one of the strongest and most courageous of the Greek warriors. He was known among his men for his intelligence and cleverness.

Behind Odysseus lay the bloody fields of battle, which had been his home for ten long years. He remembered soldiers screaming as they died, and swords and battle-axes crashing into shields. So many of his friends were dead, their lives wasted.

Now the Trojan War was over. The Greeks had beaten the Trojans. It was time for Odysseus to go home at last.

Odysseus shook his head to clear his mind of the terrible images of war. Before him lay the ocean that would carry him home to Ithaca. He longed to be home again, to stand on his native soil, to sleep in his own soft bed, to be with his wife, Penelope, and his son, Telemachus.

He stepped into the rowboat that waited to carry him to his giant ship. In just a few minutes, Odysseus boarded his vessel, looking thoughtfully at the courageous men who had survived the war. "Homeward, my friends and fellow warriors! We should be grateful that we can return to our loved ones." The crowd roared in chorus, "Homeward! Homeward, mighty Odysseus!" The anchor was lifted as the crew cheered, and Odysseus's boat set sail for home.

King Odysseus was loved by everyone. He was brave and strong, handsome and smart. His men would follow him anywhere, for they knew that with Odysseus in charge, there was nothing to fear. His courage and clever imagination could find a way out of any difficulty.

The ocean between Troy and Ithaca was very large, and it was dotted with many islands. After sailing for a little while, Odysseus and his men stopped in the land of the Lotus-eaters. After Odysseus landed, he sent three of his men out to meet the people of the island.

The Lotus-eaters had no weapons, and they

greeted Odysseus's men warmly. "We will not cause you harm. Our food is the beautiful flower that grows only on this island. Here, we offer you our sweet, magical food." The mysterious lotus plants were placed in the men's hands, and they could see that these beautiful blossoms were truly exotic and succulent. The men ate the flowers and instantly forgot their comrades and loved ones, dreaming no more of returning to Odysseus or their homelands.

Odysseus grew impatient while waiting for his men to return to the ship, so he went to look for them. Odysseus was horrified when he found them. They wanted nothing more than to live in that land forever, eating lotus blossoms all day. "Remember your homes and your families!" he told them as he began to drag the men back to the ship.

"No! Leave us here!" the men shouted, weeping bitterly.

Odysseus was forced to lock them inside the ship to keep them from staying with the Lotus-eaters. "Do not taste any of the lotus blossoms,"

Odysseus told the rest of his men. "We must leave this island quickly, or we will never see our homes again."

The crew rapidly put out to sea. They sailed for many weeks, and the men soon grew bored and tired. "Will we ever get home?" one of the sailors wondered.

"It seems like we have been on the sea forever," said another. "What I wouldn't give to walk on land again!"

"We are running out of fresh water and food," said a third sailor. "We need more supplies."

"There are many islands on the sea," Odysseus said. "We will stop at the next one. There we can find more supplies and take a short rest."

It wasn't long before an island came into view. Odysseus's crew anchored the ship in the bay. Then the king and twelve of his men boarded a small boat and rowed to shore.

The island was beautiful. Lush green plants grew everywhere, and the air was perfumed with the sweet smell of flowers. Odysseus knew that this land was the home of a strange race called the Cyclopes.

Odysseus and his men began to search the island for food and water. Finally they came to the mouth of a huge cave. From inside the cave they could smell the rich odor of delicious food— roasted meats, savory cheeses, and crusty breads.

Crazed with hunger, the sailors rushed inside the dark cave. By the light of a small fire, Odysseus saw torches mounted on the wall. He lit them, and soon the entire cave was alight. The cave was larger than they had imagined—and filled with mouth-watering food.

"Our host has seen our ship and prepared a great feast for us," Odysseus announced. On his signal, the starving sailors rushed toward the food and began to eat.

Odysseus had brought a large sack of wine from the boat to offer as a gift to his host. **It was the custom in those days for a guest to**

bring a gift when visiting someone's house. I hope they remembered gifts for the most important members of the household—the pets. He set it down on the ground and went to join his men at the feast.

Suddenly the men heard a rumbling noise. The noise grew louder and louder, and the cave began to shake. The sailors were knocked off their feet and thrown to the floor.

Odysseus struggled to his feet and staggered to the mouth of the cave. He soon saw the cause of the earthquake. Hundreds of sheep were being driven into the cave. As they stampeded inside, Odysseus ordered his men to seek shelter in the back of the cave.

A shadow loomed in the mouth of the cave. Odysseus's blood turned to ice as a hideous giant entered. His skin was a sickly shade of gray. His fingers bore huge claws, which were as sharp as swords, and his mouth was filled with fangs. Worst of all, a single yellow eye stared out from the middle of the monster's forehead. This was one of the mighty Cyclopes.

The Cyclops grabbed a huge boulder and

stuffed it into the mouth of the cave. Then he turned and saw the men hiding in the back of the cave. "Who are you?" he roared.

"We are Greeks on our way home from the Trojan War," Odysseus answered. "Please receive us as your guests, for we are hungry and tired."

The Cyclops laughed harshly. "You are fools to come here and ask for my hospitality." He picked up two of Odysseus's men and tossed them into his mouth. His sharp fangs crunched the bones of the two unfortunate sailors. He swallowed hard, and then licked his lips with his long, slimy tongue.

Odysseus's men were horrified at what had just happened to their shipmates. They cowered behind Odysseus, shaking with fear. Would one of them be next?

"I don't care who you are," the Cyclops said. "Tomorrow you will all become my dinner."

Then, with a wicked laugh, the monster lay down on the floor and fell asleep.

The sailors huddled close to Odysseus, still trembling with fear. Everyone talked at once, asking what would happen next. Odysseus knew he must calm the men quickly before their panic woke the Cyclops again. He put up his hands, motioning for silence.

"Fear not, my friends," he said. "I have a plan."

Helllooo!
Start flipping the book pages and check out the action....
Woo-cha!

4

A Clever Escape

Odysseus and his men are in a tight spot. Instead of being invited to dinner, they're about to become the main course for a one-eyed monster! Odysseus is a smart guy, though, and he's got a pretty clever trick up his sleeve to help his men escape from the horrible Cyclops.

King Odysseus did not get any sleep that night. He stayed awake to guard his men and plan the details of their escape.

Morning arrived, and the Cyclops's flock of sheep grew hungry for their breakfast. They began to bleat and snort to wake their dreadful master.

The giant Cyclops awoke. He sat up slowly, rubbing his one eye. Then he stretched his enormous arms and pushed the boulder from the mouth of the cave. Hundreds of sheep stampeded out of the cave to graze in the fields.

The Cyclops stared at Odysseus. His mighty voice rumbled through the cave. "Tonight, when I return, all of you will be my dinner," he roared. Then, laughing cruelly, he trudged outside and slammed the boulder in the opening behind him.

Seeing the trunk of a fallen tree leaning against a wall of the cave, Odysseus immediately began giving orders to seven of his men. "Take that trunk and strip the bark from it with your swords. We will sharpen one end of it into a spike." He instructed another three men to build up a fire until it was very hot.

When the giant spike was ready, the point of the tremendous weapon was put into the fire to heat. Then Odysseus explained his clever plan to the others. Just as he finished, the horrible Cyclops returned.

"And now," he roared as he replaced the boulder in the cave's mouth, "I eat my dinner!"

"Wait!" said King Odysseus. "I have not told you my name. Aren't you curious about who I am?"

"Yes, I want to know who I am eating for dinner. All right, stranger, who are you?"

"My name is No One," said Odysseus.

"No One? Well, Mr. No One, it's a pleasure to eat you." The Cyclops reached a long claw toward Odysseus.

"Wait!" cried the king.

"What now?" asked the Cyclops. "I am getting very hungry."

"You have not had any wine. Please, taste some of this excellent wine we brought from our ship."

"That sounds good to me," the Cyclops agreed. "Pour!"

Two sailors lifted the giant bowl from which

the Cyclops drank. Odysseus filled it with the
wine and the Cyclops gulped it down.

"This wine is good!" the monster shouted. "I
want more!"

Another bowl was filled and drunk as quickly
as the first.

"More!" the Cyclops cried again.

Again the bowl was filled. The wine began to do its job. The Cyclops's eye began to blur and his head began to spin. Finally the giant tumbled to the floor and fell fast asleep.

Odysseus and his men ran to the burning spike that lay within the fire. They heaved it high above their heads. Then, on the count of three, they plunged the burning point into the Cyclops's eye.

The Cyclops howled in pain. He leaped to his feet and wrenched the burning tree from his eye. Screaming, he lurched around the cave.

The shrieks of the Cyclops were so loud that all of the other Cyclopes on the island heard them. Knowing that one of their own was in trouble, they raced to the cave to see what was the matter.

"What is it?" they called. "What's wrong with you?"

"He blinded me! He blinded me!" the wounded Cyclops complained.

"Who?"

"No One blinded me! No One!"

"Well, if no one blinded you, why did you yell? Leave us alone!" With that, the other monsters went back to their homes.

Oohh! I get it. It's a play on words.

The Cyclops fumbled by the mouth of the cave and tore away the boulder. Then he sat by the entrance with his hands stretched out to grab anyone who tried to run past him and escape.

Odysseus had yet another clever plan. He quickly tied his men underneath the sheep, where they were hidden in the animals' thick wool. Odysseus saved the fattest sheep for himself. He stretched himself out beneath the animal's shaggy belly.

As the sheep ran outside, the Cyclops felt each one's back, checking for the escaping prisoners. He never guessed that the men were hidden *underneath* the sheep!

As soon as they were out of the cave,

Odysseus jumped to the ground. He cut his men free, and they all ran for their ship, taking the Cyclops's fat sheep with them.

When Odysseus and his men were safely aboard their ship, the great king could not resist taunting the monster. "Listen, Cyclops," he called. "If anyone asks who blinded you, tell them it was King Odysseus!"

Odysseus's words made the monster even more angry. If this were any other Cyclops, Odysseus would have nothing to worry about. But the monster was the son of Poseidon (poh-SY-don), the powerful god of all the oceans.

The Cyclops raised his hands toward the heavens. "Father, listen to me!" he called. "You see what Odysseus has done to your son. Grant that he never see his home again. Or, if it is your will that he does return home, may he lose all his friends on the way and find new troubles waiting for him in his own house!"

Uh-oh. It's not a good idea to tease monsters who have friends in high places! Odysseus still has many troubles to face on his journey. Will the Cyclops's curse come true?

5

The Curse of a Sorceress

After Odysseus and his men left the Cyclops's island, they sailed to an island ruled by a man named Aeolus (EE-oh-lus). Aeolus gave Odysseus an amazing gift— a bag holding the four winds. He let some of the west wind out of the bag to carry Odysseus's ship toward home.

Things went well for nine days. On the tenth night, the sailors could see the fields of their homeland in the distance. Then disaster struck.

Odysseus went to sleep early that night. For the first time in years, his heart was light. Tomorrow he would be home! He couldn't wait to see his beloved Penelope and Telemachus at long last.

Odysseus's men were also excited about being close to home. But they found themselves wondering about the mysterious bag. "I wonder what fantastic things are hidden inside it," whispered one curious sailor.

"Maybe there are jewels and gold," another sailor suggested.

"Maybe there is some sort of magical potion," guessed one more man. "Let's look and see."

"No!" cried one sailor who was more cautious than the rest. "Odysseus told us never to open the bag."

"Don't be such a worrywart," the other sailors scolded him. "What could possibly be in the bag that could hurt us?" And so, despite what they were told, the sailors opened the bag.

WHOOSH! Suddenly the air whirled around

them. The four winds rushed out of the bag in a great storm. The winds blew the ship north, then south, then east, and then west! The men were helpless and groaned bitterly against the powerful winds that were blowing the ship out to sea again, away from the homeland they had glimpsed. By the time Odysseus awoke, he and his men were far from home once more. Odysseus was so saddened to lose sight of his land that he thought he might die from grief. However, he faithfully kept his place as leader of his men and waited for the storm to calm.

At last the terrible windstorm ended. In time, Odysseus's ship came to rest on the shore of a lush, green island. The men climbed off the boat and waded to shore. Brightly colored flowers sparkled in the sunlight and filled the sailors' noses with their rich perfume.

Odysseus picked up his bow and arrows from the ship and went off to search for food. He hadn't hunted for long when a huge deer came across his path. Odysseus drew an arrow and killed the deer before it could leap away. Then he

lifted the animal upon his back and carried it to his waiting men.

The animal was roasted over a roaring fire. When the meat was ready at last, the hungry men fell upon it until there was nothing left but a pile of bones.

"Now," Odysseus said, "some of you must go and see who lives on this island."

None of the men wanted to be sent on this mission. They remembered their experience with the Cyclops and were afraid they would meet another monster. Finally a brave young soldier named Eurylochus (you-RILL-oh-kus) stepped forward.

"I will lead the mission," Eurylochus said. "Who will join me?"

Eurylochus's courage inspired his shipmates. Soon twenty-two other men joined the group. Lifting their swords, they set off into the wilderness.

The explorers walked until they reached the top of a grassy hill. From there they could look down at the center of the island. They saw a splendid palace made of smooth white stone.

In front of this beautiful palace, a lady sat working at a loom. Her hair was golden and her skin was smooth and fair. Her eyes were as green as sparkling emeralds, and her lips were the crimson of a glorious sunset. Her delicate hands moved quickly over the loom, creating a fabulous tapestry in all the colors of the rainbow. As she worked, the woman sang a tune so beautiful that it filled the listeners with joy.

In front of the lady was a silver and gold banquet table covered with food. Sweet breads, tender meats, tasty cheeses, and bowls of fruit were spread across the table.

There was one more thing to see, and this was the most amazing thing of all. The lady was surrounded by a pack of wolves and mountain lions. These were vicious animals, yet they lay

> To me, the most amazing thing is that none of the animals have gone after the food yet.

peacefully upon the ground and harmed no one.

"I think we should go down and speak to her," said one of the sailors.

Eurylochus wasn't so sure. "This is all too nice," he said. "It could be a trap."

"Don't be silly," said another sailor. "Look at all that wonderful food. I am starving!"

"We just fed heartily upon the deer," Eurylochus reminded him. "How can you be hungry?"

"I don't know, but I am," said the sailor. "I am going down to greet our hostess. Anyone who wants to join me is welcome to come along." Every single sailor followed him—except for Eurylochus.

When the men approached the lady at the loom, she rose to meet them. "Welcome," she said. "I am Circe (SIR-see), ruler of this island, which is called Aeaea (ay-EE-ah). You must be hungry. Sit around my table and enjoy my food."

No one needed to be asked again. The sailors ran to the table and attacked the food. Circe smiled and brought them a sweet drink that smelled like honey. "You must try this drink," she said as she filled their glasses. "I am very proud of it."

The men raised their glasses in a toast to Circe's health. Then they swallowed the delicious brew.

Circe pulled a golden wand from the folds of her dress and waved it over the men. Suddenly a terrible change took place. The men's bodies began to change. Their bones became shorter, their noses longer. Their hair turned into rough bristles, and their fingers and toes hardened into hooves. Odysseus's men had been changed into pigs—pigs who still had the minds of men. Circe drove the pigs into a sty and locked them inside.

Eurylochus saw all of this from his place on the hill. Horrified, he ran back to the harbor to tell Odysseus what had happened.

Circe is one bad goddess! Only Odysseus can save his men from her wicked spell. Is he strong enough to challenge such a powerful witch?

6
Help from High Places

Remember how Athena stepped in to help Telemachus search for his father? Odysseus could use that kind of help in his fight against Circe. And he's about to get it from Hermes (HER-meez), the messenger god!

Eurylochus ran back to the boat as fast as he could. He found Odysseus hard at work repairing some damage to his ship. As soon as Odysseus saw Eurylochus, he knew something was very wrong.

Gasping for breath, Eurylochus told his terrible tale. Odysseus was furious when he heard what had happened to his men. He was ready to set off in search of Circe, but Eurylochus begged him not to go.

"Glorious captain," the sailor begged, "the men are lost. Nothing can be done to save them. Do not allow the witch to capture you as well!"

"I cannot leave my men to suffer such an awful fate," Odysseus told him. "Don't worry. I do not intend to be captured by this witch!" With that, Odysseus picked up his mighty sword and headed into the wilderness.

Meanwhile, someone was watching all of this from the top of Mount Olympus, home of the gods. The watcher was Hermes, the messenger god. He knew that Odysseus could never succeed against a witch as powerful as Circe. Odysseus needed help—and Hermes intended to give it.

Strapping on his winged sandals, Hermes leaped from Mount Olympus. Bouncing off a cloud and sliding down a rainbow, he soon landed on Circe's island.

As Odysseus stepped into a clearing in the woods, he saw a marvelous sight—a boy dressed in gold, surrounded by dancing light. He bowed down before the god, and Hermes began to speak:

"Beware! For in that house lies harm,
Oh, mighty king of many men.
And if you go without my charm,
You never shall see home again.
But I can offer you my aid
And keep you safe from Circe's power,
For here within this very glade
There grows a potent magic flower.
Hold fast this flower in your hand
And when you drink from Circe's wine
Her magic will not work as planned
And you shall not be turned to swine."

Why is Hermes talking in rhyme? Actually, all of THE ODYSSEY was created in rhyme. Poems are easy to remember and recite. That was very important for THE ODYSSEY, which was spoken rather than written down.

Hermes bent down and picked a purple flower from the ground. He handed the blossom to Odysseus, and then disappeared into the sky.

Odysseus held tight to the flower and offered up silent thanks to Hermes. Then he continued on his way.

At last he reached the hill where poor Eurylochus had stood and watched the witch turn his friends into pigs. Odysseus looked down on the same beautiful scene that had greeted his men: the beautiful golden-haired lady at her loom, surrounded by peaceful animals, before a table laden with food.

As Odysseus approached, Circe rose. "Welcome to my island, handsome traveler," the witch said. "You look weary and hungry. Join me at my table and share my food."

"Thank you," Odysseus said, still clutching the flower, "but I am not hungry."

"Then you must try my honey wine," Circe insisted. "I will not take no for an answer." She filled a cup with the sweet drink and handed it to Odysseus. He drank it, but the magic of the flower did its work. The drink had no effect on him.

"Now you will see what fate falls on all strangers who trespass on my island!" Circe shouted. She pulled out her golden wand and waved it in the air, but nothing happened.

"Who are you that you aren't affected by my magic?" a shocked Circe demanded.

"I am Odysseus," the king said. He pulled his sword and laid the point against Circe's slender neck. "Release my men," he demanded, and led her to the pigsty.

Circe had no choice but to do as Odysseus asked. She waved her wand over the pigs. Instantly they were changed back into men.

"Now swear to me that you will never use your magic to harm me, my boat, or my men," Odysseus demanded. He knew that when a witch made an oath, she was bound to it forever.

"I swear it," Circe said. Odysseus put his sword away.

Believe it or not, after Odysseus rescued his men from Circe's power, the two became very good friends. Life on

the island became so wonderful that many of the sailors would have been happy to stay there forever. And so they stayed...and stayed...and stayed. A whole year went by.

One day, Odysseus went walking on the beach. He was very homesick, and he missed his wife and son very much. He felt that it was time to return to the ones he loved on Ithaca, his beautiful homeland. He thought dreamily of the sounds and smells he would once again know upon his return. His desire to return home was so great that his yearnings made him weary. His heart ached, and he cried tears of grief, wishing he could begin his journey back home. He approached Circe to tell her of his decision.

"Odysseus," said Circe, "I know that you want to return home. But first you have to make another voyage. You must go down to Hades (HAY-deez), the Land of the Dead. **In Greek legends, Hades is where people's spirits went when they died. As you can imagine, it wasn't a place anyone wanted to visit!**

There you must talk with the blind seer Tiresias (ty-REEZ-ee-us). He will tell you what the future holds."

Odysseus was heartbroken by this new delay in reaching his home. He feared that Circe's demand that he go to Hades might be dangerous. He knew that no boat had ever been able to reach Hades. Still, he knew Circe's plan could help him on his journey home. So he listened to her directions that would take him to the deep waters of the ocean and the low shores where trees let drop their dying fruit. Then he returned to his ship and prepared for his unearthly journey.

7
The Land of the Dead

You'd think Odysseus might make up some excuse not to go to Hades. I mean, we are talking about the Land of the Dead! Helllooo! But the brave warrior Odysseus is always ready to do what must be done to get home.

Hades was a grim world. The sun never shone there, and all was dark, gloomy, and cold. The souls of the dead haunted this land, floating through its barren fields and leafless trees like the ghosts they were.

Odysseus left his boat and his men on the shores of the River Styx (STICKS). He sat down to wait for Tiresias, the blind seer who now lived in the Land of the Dead.

While Odysseus waited, he was surrounded by many ghosts, all wailing and crying. Odysseus ignored them. They were not the ones he had come to see.

Odysseus waited a long time. At last Tiresias came and stood beside him. "We never see living men walk in this land," Tiresias said in surprise. "Why have you left the light of day to come among the dead?"

"I have come to hear your words, great prophet," Odysseus answered. "I am on a long journey home. Tell me what will happen to me."

A prophet is someone who tells the future. Think how handy that would be around dinnertime.

"Great Odysseus, all you desire is to go home," Tiresias told him. "You will suffer many hardships along the way. Poseidon is angry at you because you blinded his son, the Cyclops. Soon you will travel to Trinacria (trin-AYK-ree-ah), the island of Helios (HEE-lee-ohs), the sun god. You and your crew must not touch his cattle. If you do, your ship and all your crew will be destroyed."

"Can you tell me about those who are waiting for me at home?" Odysseus asked.

"There is much wrong in your house," Tiresias told him. "Cruel men are there, wasting your food and tormenting your wife and son. When you return, you must seek revenge against them to restore peace to your home."

Odysseus was troubled by all that Tiresias had said. "Why should my family have to suffer?" he asked himself. "I should be there to protect them. I must get home!"

Just then, one of the ghosts drew closer. Odysseus was stunned to see that it was the ghost of his mother. "Mother, what are you doing here?" he asked. "You were alive when I left Ithaca to go to war."

Odysseus's mother sighed. "My son, I missed you so much that I died of a broken heart. Things are not well at home. Your wife weeps day and night, and your son cannot help her. Your father, Laertes, lives in the fields and refuses to go into town. He sleeps on the ground, grieving for you and longing for your return."

Odysseus was greatly saddened by his mother's words. Three times he tried to take her in his arms and hug her, but each time she slipped through his arms like a shadow.

"Dear mother, why won't you let me embrace you?" Odysseus cried at last. "I want to help ease your sorrow."

"When we are dead, our souls fly free and our bodies are no more. Now it is time for you to

Whew! Hades is a gloomy place. Not on my list of favorite hangouts. I'm glad Odysseus is out of there. What lies in store for our hero next?

go back to your own world. Hurry away from here, and keep in mind all I have told you," his mother said sadly.

Odysseus did as she told him. Hurrying to his ship, he commanded his men to row back up the River Styx, back to the land of the living.

8
Danger!

Odysseus is more determined than ever to get back home now. He just makes a quick stop back on Circe's island to get supplies, and then he and his crew are ready to put out to sea again.

As Odysseus's men prepared to leave their island paradise, Odysseus went to say good-bye to Circe.

"If you must leave now, I will not stop you," said Circe. "In fact, I'll give you some advice. Many dangers lie in store for you upon your journey. First you will pass the land of the Sirens. These beautiful women sing a song so lovely that any man who hears it is drawn to them—and to his death."

"How can we escape this terrible fate?" Odysseus asked.

"You must fill the ears of all your men with wax so they cannot hear the Sirens' song," Circe advised him. "As for yourself, order your men to tie you to the mast. No matter how much you beg them, they must not let you go to the Sirens' land."

"What other dangers wait for us?"

"After you pass the Sirens, you will come to a stretch of water between two mighty cliffs. On one cliff lives Scylla (SILL-ah), a monster with twelve feet, six necks, and six heads. Each head bears three rows of sharp teeth. No ship can pass by Scylla without some members of the crew being snatched up in the monster's awful jaws.

"Below the other cliff dwells another monster, Charybdis (kah-RIB-dis). She draws the water down so fast that any ship nearby is sucked to its destruction. It would be better to pass Scylla and lose just six men, rather than lose everything to Charybdis."

"Isn't there a way I can defeat them both?" asked Odysseus.

"Must you always think of battle?" asked Circe with a gentle smile. "No, my friend, you cannot defeat them both."

Odysseus took Circe's hand and said good-bye. Then, still thinking of her warnings, he returned to his men. They boarded their ship and set out at last for home.

For several weeks, everything went well. Then one day the sailors heard a beautiful melody floating on the breeze. The tune was so lovely that the men immediately turned the ship toward it.

Odysseus remembered Circe's warning. "This is the music of the Sirens," he told his crew. "You must do exactly as I say or all is lost. Fill your ears with wax so you cannot hear the Sirens' song. Then tie me firmly to the mast with good strong rope. In this way, we can safely pass the Sirens."

The sailors did as they were told. The ship drew closer to the land, and the splendor of the Sirens' music flowed over Odysseus. It was the most beautiful sound he had ever heard. Every muscle in his body strained toward it, yet the ropes bound him helplessly to his ship.

Odysseus longed for the music so much that he temporarily lost his mind. "You must let me down!" he cried, and fought the ropes, moaning and screaming. "Untie me!" he begged his men. "Let me go to the Sirens! Please!" He twisted and kicked to free himself of the ropes, but his men would not release him. Instead they tied him tighter to the mast, giving him no chance to escape and steer the ship to land. Finally, exhausted, Odysseus fainted.

The ship sailed on. The salty breeze blew over Odysseus and soon revived him. His good sense was with him again as the land of the Sirens disappeared into the distance.

Once past the danger of the Sirens, the ship traveled on. It came upon the narrow stretch of water between two cliffs. Odysseus recalled what Circe had said about this place.

The ship slid smoothly between the cliffs. Halfway through, Odysseus saw a gaping whirlpool on one side. Roaring and bubbling, the whirlpool sucked the water down. Odysseus had never seen anything like it. This was the home of Charybdis; she caused a whirlpool so powerful that even a bird flying overhead would be sucked from the sky and into its watery depths.

The ship began to spin toward the deadly pool. "Turn to starboard!" Odysseus roared at his crew. "Turn toward the opposite cliff!"

The oarsmen struggled. Soon the ship turned away from the deadly whirlpool and continued its journey along the base of the other cliff.

Odysseus hardly had a chance to catch his breath when a piercing screech rang out from above. Everyone looked upward at the sound, and their eyes beheld a horrible sight. Leaning out from a cave in the cliff was the monster Scylla: a creature with a scaly body and six necks as thick as tree trunks and as long as the ship itself. On the end of every neck was a green and slimy head armed with flashing fangs. The six heads shrieked as the necks slithered about like pythons. Then the twelve

Major uh-oh!

flaming eyes focused on Odysseus's ship.

"Full speed ahead!" Odysseus shouted. Every oar dipped quickly into the water, but nothing could move fast enough to get away. Scylla's six heads dropped like lightning toward the boat, and each head, bearing three rows of sharp teeth, snatched a man in its jaws.

Odysseus drew his sword, but he was too late. The men who were grabbed screamed for help, but poor Odysseus could only watch as Scylla gulped them down.

The boat raced on, fighting desperately to reach the end of this deadly strait. Scylla reared her heads and bent toward the ship for a second time. The oarsmen pushed hard against the water. Just in time, they passed from Scylla's reach and shot out into the open sea.

The crewmen were stunned at the loss of their companions. Odysseus walked among them, comforting them as best he could, even though his own heart was heavy. "We must sail on," he told them.

Next Odysseus and his men came to the

island of the sun. They could see flocks of sheep and herds of cattle roaming there, all belonging to the god Helios. Odysseus recalled the words of Tiresias, the seer in the Land of the Dead.

"We must not set foot on this island," Odysseus told his crew. "A terrible fate awaits us if we do."

The men were angry and upset at having to pass by such a beautiful place. "Odysseus, you are the strongest of men," said Eurylochus. "Nothing tires you. Yet we are exhausted and hungry. Can't we just spend one night here on the beach?"

Odysseus knew he should say no, but he saw how tired and hungry his men were. "All right," he agreed reluctantly. "We can camp here. But we must eat only the stores of food on our ship. Promise me you will not harm or eat any animal on this island."

The men quickly agreed. That night, however, a storm blew in and stranded everyone on land. For a whole month, the wind raged. Wild gusts blew across the island for many days.

Up from the south and the east, the forceful breath from the sky kept coming. Soon all the food on the ship was gone and the men began to starve.

Odysseus went off by himself to pray to the gods to save his crew. While he was gone, Eurylochus gathered the men around him.

"Odysseus has told us that terrible things will happen if we eat any of the cattle on this island. I say that any death is hateful, but starving to death is the worst of all. Let us eat some of the cattle that are so plentiful here."

The crew agreed. By the time Odysseus returned, his men had already killed and eaten one of the oxen.

Odysseus was full of sorrow and dread when he approached the shore and ship. He could smell the roasting meat that he had forbidden the men to eat. He dreaded the consequences and called out his fear for the harm that might come to them.

The next day, the weather cleared. Odysseus and his men hurried onto their ship and sailed away from Helios's island. But they could not escape the god's anger.

No sooner were the men at sea when a terrible storm struck the ship. Wind and rain pounded the sea, destroying everything in their path. Odysseus's ship was helpless in the face of this storm. Torn and twisted by the waves, the ship smashed into a jagged rock. It cracked and splintered until nothing was left but a few scraps of wood.

The air was filled with screams of terror as the sailors plunged into the raging ocean. Men clawed helplessly at the water, only to sink beneath it and drown. There was no escape—every member of the crew was lost except Odysseus.

Odysseus fought desperately to keep his head above water. Gasping for breath, he plunged beneath the waves, then kicked his way to the surface once more. Finally a plank of wood—all that was left of his once-mighty ship—floated near him. Odysseus grabbed it and held on with all his strength. The winds continued to rage as he rode on the wild ocean, all alone amid the ever-rising and crashing waves.

Half-drowned and exhausted, his ship destroyed, and his crew dead, Odysseus drifted, on the waters of the endless ocean.

Now Odysseus has lost everything—except his life. And his problems aren't over yet. Another obstacle awaits him—one that is much gentler than the stormy sea, but no less dangerous.

9
Prisoner of a Goddess

Odysseus didn't float
on the sea forever. He
finally washed up on
the shore of an island
called Ogygia (oh-JIJ-ee-ah). This
island was the home of the
goddess Calypso (kah-LIP-so). Didn't I
say before that all the gods and
goddesses lived on Mount Olympus? Well, most
of them did. But Calypso was different. No one
knew why, but she preferred to live alone upon
Ogygia. And she's about to get her claws into our
hero.

The plank of wood that was all that was left of Odysseus's ship finally came to rest upon the shore. The mighty king lay senseless, worn out from his ordeal.

Finally Odysseus awoke. "I am so hungry," he mumbled, feeling the empty ache in his belly.

He had no sooner spoken than a blazing fire appeared beside him. Over it hung a wild boar on a spit. Odysseus was so hungry that he didn't even stop to think where this food might have come from. He immediately flung himself on the roasting meat and gobbled up every bit of it.

After Odysseus had eaten, he slowly stood up and looked around. Suddenly, the truth of what had happened struck him, and he was overwhelmed by sorrow. "I am cursed! Why has such misfortune found me?" he moaned. "All my men are dead and I am far from home." Tears ran down his cheeks as he wept for his lost men and his own fate.

"Do not cry," said a sweet voice behind him. "I will take care of you."

Odysseus turned and beheld the most beautiful woman he had ever seen. **Hello! Let's**

see.... A strange island, good food, and a beautiful woman. But they are not what they seem. Can you spell D-A-N-G-E-R? Her hair was long and flamed as red as the sunset, and her face was fair and flawless.

"My name is Odysseus," the king said at last. "I am trying to return to my home on Ithaca, but I was shipwrecked in a storm and washed ashore on this island."

"I know all of your troubles, for I have much power," said Calypso. "You see, I am a goddess, and I know everything."

"Then you will help me return home?" Odysseus asked in excitement. For the first time since landing there, he dared to hope.

"A goddess can do anything she pleases," Calypso told him. "It does not please me to allow you to return home."

Odysseus thought his heart would break at her words. "Why won't you help me?" he asked.

"Because I am fond of you. I shall keep you here for company."

"For how long?" Odysseus was almost afraid to ask.

"For as long as I want to," Calypso snapped. She was growing angry. "Beware, Odysseus, for I can be as wicked as I can be helpful. You do not want to cross me!" Her eyes flashed fire, and Odysseus shivered in fear.

So Odysseus became a prisoner of the goddess Calypso. He wept bitterly and longed to go home. His imprisonment lasted for seven long years.

Seven years! I'd hate to be on a leash for that long.

10
Free at Last

Odysseus still has some waiting to do. While he's trapped on Calypso's island, our story travels up to Mount Olympus, where the goddess Athena is talking to Zeus, king of all the gods.

The golden palace of the gods glittered upon the highest peak of Mount Olympus. Precious gems gleamed from the walls. The floors were of purest marble and the windows of finest crystal. The castle was so beautiful that any mortal who looked at it would go blind instantly.

In the center of all this splendor sat the throne of almighty Zeus. From here, the king of all the gods could gaze upon the earth and shower it with blessings—or wave a finger and destroy it all.

Today Zeus sat quietly upon his throne. His thick white hair fell heavily around his handsome face, and his long beard flowed smoothly from his chin. His eyes gleamed with the sparkling light of heaven.

Before Zeus stood Athena, the goddess of wisdom and the champion of Odysseus. She had been born full-grown from the head of Zeus, and she was the favorite of his many children.

"Father," Athena said, "look down at Ogygia, the island of Calypso, and see how Odysseus suffers as her prisoner. For seven years now, she has kept him there against his will. Take pity on him, Father, and allow him to return to Ithaca in safety."

Zeus gazed down upon Ogygia and saw Odysseus lost in sorrow upon the shore. "Athena, you are right," he said. "Odysseus has suffered enough. It has always been my will that he return home one day. Now that time has come."

Athena smiled with happiness. Zeus called Hermes, messenger of the gods, and sent him to Ogygia to tell Calypso what she must do.

"Thank you, Father," said Athena. "Now I shall travel to Sparta, where Telemachus is seeking news of his father. I shall tell him to return home. It will take both Telemachus and his father to rid the palace of the evil suitors." Then, bowing low before the king of all the gods, Athena vanished.

Meanwhile, Hermes winged his way to Calypso's island. He found the goddess resting in the cave where she made her home.

"Hermes," Calypso said in surprise. "I did not expect you. It's been a long time since you visited me. Come, have a meal with me."

Instantly a table full of sweet ambrosia and delicious nectar appeared before Hermes. **Ambrosia was the food of the gods. I've never tried it personally,**

but if it's good enough for the gods, then it's good enough for this cute little dog. Hermes and Calypso ate and drank together. When they had finished, Calypso asked, "What news do you bring me, Hermes?"

"I bring a command from Zeus himself," Hermes told her. "He demands that you set Odysseus free."

Calypso was furious. "Who is he to meddle in my affairs?" she shouted angrily.

"Who is he?" Hermes echoed. "He is the king of the gods, and his wrath is terrible. You do not want to make him angry."

Calypso knew this was true. "All right," she said sullenly. "He may go."

"Zeus also commands that you tell Odysseus that he is free, and swear you will not hurt him," Hermes told her. "You must also help him build a raft upon which he will leave this island." His message delivered, Hermes said good-bye to Calypso and vanished in a golden spray of mist.

Calypso knew she had no choice but to do as Zeus wanted. She found Odysseus sitting on the shore. He was staring toward Ithaca, dreaming of his journey home.

"Odysseus," Calypso told him, "the time has come for you to leave. I will help you build a raft, and you shall sail home."

Odysseus did not believe her. "You have kept me a prisoner for seven years," he said warily. "Why do you release me now? Are you planning some awful revenge on me when I leave your island?"

"No, Odysseus," said Calypso. "I swear that I will not hurt you. Zeus himself has commanded that I set you free, and so I must do it."

For the first time in seven years, Odysseus's heart was filled with happiness. The sparkle returned to his eyes, and his face broke into a grin as he shouted for joy. Soon he would see his Penelope and Telemachus, whom he had longed to be with for years. How good it would feel to at last set foot on the ground of Ithaca. He was going home!

Odysseus's journey is almost at an end. Odysseus, however, still has a few more problems to face before his trip is over. Turn the page!

11
Shipwrecked!

Calypso gave Odysseus an axe and the other tools that he needed to build a raft. With mighty blows, Odysseus felled giant trees. Then he stripped and shaped them, and fitted them into a sturdy raft. He worked for four long days. On the fifth day, he said good-bye to Calypso and set out on the ocean.

Odysseus sailed for seventeen days. On the eighteenth day, he came in sight of the land of Phaeacia (fe-AY-sha), lying dark upon the water like a shield.

It was then that Poseidon, god of the seas, saw Odysseus sailing along. The god remembered the terrible wound Odysseus had given his son, the Cyclops, and he grew very angry. "Odysseus may be close to home," the sea god said to himself, "but I will see that he suffers even more before he gets there!

"How can it be that you sail within my kingdom and you do not worry, though you have so violently wounded my son?" Poseidon bellowed. His wrath echoed across the sea.

Poseidon called to the clouds around him and woke the ocean. The black ocean swelled as

Poseidon shook with anger. The wind began to blow, and towering waves rolled over the sea. Poseidon unleashed the full fury of his storm right over Odysseus's raft.

"You are still trying to keep me from reaching my homeland?" Odysseus called out to the hurricanes that crashed upon him. "I have lived through many dangers, but how many more disasters can I endure?" He trembled from the thought and clung more fiercely to his raft as the storm broke over him. He struggled to breathe as waves washed over his head. Far away, he caught a glimpse of land. "I must swim for the shore," Odysseus decided. "It is my only hope."

Odysseus dove into the waves. For two days and nights he struggled through the mighty waves. Finally, on the third day, he reached land of Phaeacia and was able to crawl ashore. Then, exhausted from his ordeal, he curled up on the ground and fell asleep.

The goddess Athena had been watching Odysseus as he sailed on his raft. She knew he would reach the coast of Phaeacia, lost and all alone, and would need someone to help him.

So Athena appeared in a dream to Nausicaä (naw-SIK-ay-ah), the kind-hearted daughter of the Phaeacian king and queen. "You have such magnificent robes, but have neglected them," Athena said in the dream. "Your marriage day is not far off, and yet you do not care for these garments. Before the dawn, you must go to wash them, for you will not remain unwed for much longer." Athena knew that when Nausicaä went to wash her robes she would be sure to find Odysseus.

Very early the next morning, Nausicaä went down to the water with her companions to wash her robes. When she reached the shore, she dreamily began washing, unaware of anything around her. One of her companions tossed a ball to her, but she did not notice. When the ball splashed in the water before her, she shrieked with surprise.

Odysseus was startled from his sleep. He had been lying amid some bushes. He felt sore all over, and his dry body was covered with the ocean's salty dust. He knew he looked ragged and worn, but when he saw Nausicaä, he knew he must talk to her. Standing slowly, he walked calmly toward the Phaeacian girl. She stood back from this wild-looking man, but she was not afraid.

"Who are you, and what are you doing here?" Nausicaä asked.

"I am Odysseus, King of Ithaca. For ten years I fought in the Trojan War. In the ten years since the war's end, I have been trying to get home to my wife and son on Ithaca. Many terrible things have happened to me along the way. I have been held prisoner by a goddess, and my men have all been killed. All I want is to get home!"

"My parents are the king and queen of this land," Nausicaä told him. "Come to the palace with me. I'm sure they will help you."

The king and queen welcomed Odysseus and honored him as their guest. In return for the hospitality, Odysseus told them of all his adventures, from his meeting with the Cyclops to the horrible encounter with Scylla and

Charybdis, from the terrifying storms to his long imprisonment on Calypso's island.

Princess Nausicaä was weeping when Odysseus finished his story, and the others in the audience were also greatly moved at the traveler's tale.

"You have suffered much, my friend," said the Phaeacian king. "Now you shall go home in safety."

Those were the sweetest words Odysseus had heard in a long time. "I can never thank you enough," he said to the king. "Going home is my fondest dream. May the gods bless you for helping it come true!"

The next morning, a crew of Phaeacian nobleman boarded a mighty ship to escort Odysseus home. People gathered on the shore to bid good-bye to their guest and wish him a safe journey.

Odysseus was overjoyed to be going home. But he was also exhausted from all that he had gone through. When the boat at last arrived on Ithaca's shore, Odysseus was fast asleep. The crew did not want to interrupt his rest, so they carried him gently to the shore and laid him down beneath the shade of an olive tree. There they left him to finish his dreams in peace.

Odysseus may be on his home shore at last, but whatever happened to Telemachus? He's got a journey of his own to make, and there's still a lot to do before Odysseus can enjoy his "home, sweet home."

12
A Joyful Reunion

While King Odysseus made his way to Ithaca from Calypso's island, his son, Telemachus, had arrived at the palace of King Menelaus of Sparta.

Telemachus and his companions had reached the land where Menelaus lived. Once at the gate and standing at the entrance to the beautiful palace, Telemachus was welcomed in to the wedding feast that was being held for Menelaus's daughter. He was brought in to sit with the other guests, given a pitcher of water for his hands, and offered a share from the banquet of food. When he heard Menelaus speak to his guests of his beloved dead comrades whom he fought with at Troy, and of his respect for

Odysseus, who had been lost for many years, tears pooled in Telemachus's eyes. Then he spoke directly to Menelaus.

"I have come from Ithaca for a private matter. I am here to ask you about my noble father, Odysseus."

Menelaus noticed the resemblance. "Your father was a great friend of mine. I have known no other warrior as brave and heroic as he. I would be glad to tell you what I know. Recently I was told by an old friend that your father was last seen on the island of Calypso." Then the king invited Telemachus to stay in his palace.

Later that night, Telemachus went to bed in King Menelaus's palace. He lay there but could not sleep. His mind was filled with thoughts of his father. Would he ever find him?

Just then, the goddess Athena appeared beside his bed. "Telemachus," she told him, "it is time for you to go home. You must sail only at night, for some of the suitors are planning to kill you. When you reach Ithaca's shore, go to the hut of the swineherd Eumaeus (yoo-MEE-us). You

A swineherd is someone who cares for a herd of pigs.

must spend the night there if all is to come out right."

As soon as morning came, Telemachus hurried to do as he was told. He went to Menelaus. "I must return to my own home," he told the king. "Things are in a terrible state there because of the suitors tormenting my mother. I must go home and take charge of things once and for all."

"I understand," Menelaus said. He gave Telemachus many gifts to bring back to Ithaca, and saw the young prince on his way.

Meanwhile, Athena's work was not yet finished. After she appeared to Telemachus, she traveled to Ithaca to greet Odysseus.

When Odysseus woke, at first he wasn't sure where he was. Suddenly a golden light appeared before him. Athena stepped out of the light, and Odysseus bowed before her.

"Rise, Odysseus," the goddess said. "Your wanderings are over."

Odysseus sank to his knees and kissed the ground. He was home at last! The land of Ithaca—his land—was truly the sweetest thing he had seen in all his travels. Odysseus was so happy that tears filled his eyes.

"Do not rejoice yet," Athena warned him. "All is not well at your house. Your hall is filled with evil suitors. They are destroying your property and wasting your stores of food. Worst of all, they torment your wife, Penelope, in an effort to get her to marry one of them. You must stop them before there is nothing left to save."

When Odysseus heard her words, he grew hot with rage. "Great goddess, you must help me battle the suitors and restore peace to my house," he said.

"I will help you," Athena promised. "First you must go to Eumaeus, your swineherd. There you will rest until your son, Telemachus, joins you."

"Telemachus—my son!" Odysseus was overcome with emotion at the thought of seeing

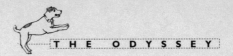

his son. Telemachus had been just an infant when Odysseus left home. Now he was a man.

"Go quickly, Odysseus," Athena said.

"How am I to know if Eumaeus is faithful to me?" Odysseus asked. "What if he betrays me to the suitors?"

"I will disguise you as a hungry old beggar. In that disguise, you may test him as you see fit."

Athena waved a hand before Odysseus. Instantly he was transformed into an elderly beggar. Then the goddess disappeared, and Odysseus set off to Eumaeus's hut.

When Odysseus reached the hut, Eumaeus welcomed him and gave him everything a visitor deserved: food, clean clothing, and a place to sleep. Then Eumaeus asked him, "Who are you and where do you come from?"

Odysseus was not ready to reveal his true identity. Instead he said, "Twenty years ago, I left to fight the war in Troy. On the voyage home, I was attacked by pirates who stole all I had. They would have made a slave of me, but I escaped. Since then, I have wandered the world as you see me now."

Eumaeus was moved by the stranger's story. "My beloved master, King Odysseus, also went to Troy to fight the war. He never made it home again."

Odysseus was pleased to hear himself spoken of so respectfully by Eumaeus. He decided to test the swineherd.

"This king of yours must be dead by now," Odysseus said. "Doesn't that free you from your duty to him?"

"Indeed, I fear the king will never return. My heart grows heavy even to speak of him, for he was a great man. Still, I hope I am wrong and he does return someday."

Odysseus was glad to hear his faithful friend honor him. He was just about to reveal his true identity when a man stepped up to the doorway. "Telemachus," Eumaeus called out with surprise. "It is so good to see you again after your long travels. I have missed you, as I do your great father."

Telemachus was relieved to have finally made his way to Eumaeus's hut. He had returned to help his mother, though he still did not understand why Athena had sent him to Eumaeus first.

Odysseus stared in wonder at this tall, handsome man. He was overwhelmed with pride to think that this was his son.

"Please, Eumaeus, will you go to my mother and tell her I am safely back home?" Telemachus requested. "I know she has been worried about me while I was gone."

Eumaeus hurried to do as Telemachus asked. When Telemachus and Odysseus were alone, Odysseus stared at his son for a long time. Finally he spoke.

"I know why Athena sent you here," he told his son.

Telemachus was startled. "Are you mocking Athena?" he asked.

"No, I am not mocking her," Odysseus told him. "Look!" Instantly, Odysseus was bathed in golden light. When the glow faded, Odysseus no longer looked like an aged beggar. He was once again in his true form.

Telemachus stared in wonder at the handsome, rugged man before him. "Father?" he whispered at last, hardly daring to believe the truth.

"My son," Odysseus said proudly.

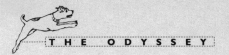

Telemachus threw his arms around his father and burst into tears. Odysseus wept too because he was so happy to see his son again.

At last the two drew apart. "How is your mother, Penelope?" Odysseus asked. "Is she well? Has she been true to me for all these years?"

"Penelope longs for nothing more than your return," Telemachus told his father. "But the suitors torment her daily. We must defeat them and drive them from the house."

This is great! Group hug, everybody!

"Here is what we shall do," Odysseus told his son. "You must go home and secretly remove the weapons from the hall, so the suitors will be unarmed. Hide two sharp swords for us to use. That way we will have the advantage."

"Father," Telemachus said, "there are one hundred suitors and only two of us. Can we really hope to defeat them?"

"Fear not, my son," Odysseus assured him. "We will triumph."

The moment of truth is almost at hand. Soon Odysseus and Telemachus will confront the suitors. Then we'll see who's top dog!

13
In Disguise

**Odysseus decides to see
for himself what is going
on at home. He's about to
have some interesting
experiences talking to people who
don't know who he really is.**

Later that day, Eumaeus, Telemachus, and
Odysseus, again disguised as a beggar, went
to the palace. As they came near the door, a
dog lying outside suddenly pricked up its ears.

This was Argus, Odysseus's dog. Argus had only been a puppy when Odysseus left to fight in the Trojan War. Now he was old and sick.

As Odysseus drew closer, Argus's tail began to wag. He tried to greet his old master, but could not make it to his feet. Odysseus was moved by the sight of his old dog.

"That dog belonged to King Odysseus," Eumaeus told him. "In his prime, he was the fastest and strongest dog on Ithaca. But no one cares for him now, and he has suffered greatly." Then Eumaeus led Odysseus inside.

Argus watched them go. Then, happy at finally having seen his beloved master after twenty long years, Argus died.

Inside Odysseus's hall, Antinous was singing and banging on the table with a metal cup. The other suitors laughed and clapped as Antinous stood up to dance. He wobbled on his clumsy feet and fell backward, crashing onto a banquet table piled high with food. Bread and meat flew everywhere as Antinous tumbled to the floor.

Still playing the part of a beggar, Odysseus went around the room asking for scraps of meat and bread. Most of the suitors gave him something—except for Antinous.

"Who let this beggar in here?" Antinous roared. "Don't we have enough pests asking for handouts already?"

"Antinous, you shouldn't speak that way," Eumaeus scolded him. "No one ever invites the poor to a feast, but they need to eat too."

"That's right," put in Telemachus. "I will not allow you to drive this stranger from my door."

Antinous was so angry at what Eumaeus and Telemachus told him that he picked up his footstool and hit Odysseus on the back with it. Odysseus didn't move under the blow. He only shook his head and said, "Listen, all you suitors! Antinous struck me only because I am hungry. May the gods strike him down someday!"

"Oh, be quiet," Antinous grumbled. "Eat in peace, or I will have you dragged from the house."

That night Penelope came down from her room. When she heard there was a stranger in the hall, she asked to see him. "Poor beggar," she said, "I have heard that you have traveled far. Have you any news of my husband, King Odysseus?"

Odysseus longed to tell Penelope who he really was, but he knew that the right time had not yet come. Instead he made up a story about how he had met Odysseus and his men on their journey.

Penelope was moved by his words. "Dear guest, I thank you for your news," she said. "Let my nurse wash your feet, for I know they are dusty and tired from your days on the road." Before Odysseus could refuse, Penelope called Eurycleia (yoo-re-KLEE-ah), the elderly nurse who had cared for Odysseus as he was growing up. The nurse was an honored member of the household.

Eurycleia studied Odysseus carefully as she knelt before him. "We have had many guests here over the years," she said, "but I have never seen anyone who looks and sounds so much like Odysseus, our absent king."

"Oh, yes," Odysseus said, thinking quickly. "People are always telling me that Odysseus and I look alike."

Eurycleia took one of Odysseus's feet into her hands to wash it. Then, startled, she dropped it, knocking over her bowl and spilling water all over the floor. She could hardly believe her eyes. There on the beggar's foot was a scar exactly like one Odysseus bore!

Tears filled the old nurse's eyes as she touched Odysseus on the cheek. "You are King Odysseus," she said with great emotion. "I knew you as soon as I saw that scar."

She turned to call Penelope to her side, but Odysseus stopped her. "No," he said. "Don't tell anyone yet. I must keep my identity a secret if I am to defeat the suitors."

"All right," Eurycleia reluctantly agreed. "Just don't wait too long. It is long past the time for you to regain your rightful place!"

Whew! That was a close call! Odysseus is just about ready to make his move. What will happen when he and the suitors finally face each other in battle?

14
The Challenge

Penelope has had about all she can take of the suitors. She'll do just about anything to get rid of them. Fortunately, she's about to get some help from our old friend Athena.

It was late when Penelope returned to her room. She shuddered at the noise below. If only there were some way to chase the suitors from her house!

The goddess Athena had just such a plan in mind. She put the idea into Penelope's head to declare a very special contest.

Inspired by Athena, Penelope went to a corner of the room and picked up the bow of King Odysseus. It was his favorite weapon, and any arrow he shot from it flew straight and true. For twenty years, no one had drawn this bow because there was no string on it. Penelope knew that only Odysseus was strong enough to bend the bow and string it.

Penelope found a string and carried the bow downstairs. For the first time, hope rose in her heart. This bow would provide the perfect contest for her hand in marriage!

Penelope descended gracefully into the hall. The suitors fell quiet when they saw her. The queen held up the bow and announced, "Look upon the bow of the great Odysseus, your king. He who bends this bow and strings it shall be my new husband. If no one here can do that, I will marry none of you."

The suitors cried out in protest. "Anyone can

string a bow!" they shouted. "That isn't any contest. It's much too easy!"

"Then I'll make it harder," Penelope said. "We will set up twelve axes in a row on their handles. The man who can shoot an arrow through the holes of all twelve after he has strung the bow shall become my husband."

Antinous roared his approval. "This is a contest worthy of my greatness. I promise you, Penelope, I shall be the winner. And then I will be your husband!"

Penelope shivered at the thought.

The hall erupted with activity as everyone prepared for the contest. Twelve sharp axes were placed on their handles, and the tiny holes in their blades were lined up in a row. A servant brought in a quiver full of arrows and placed it on the ground before the axes.

Meanwhile, the suitors stretched and flexed their hands in preparation for the contest. While they were busy, Telemachus and Eumaeus secretly removed the weapons from the hall as Odysseus had instructed. They also hid two swords by the door.

Finally the contest began. A suitor named Leiodes (lie-OH-deez) was the first to try, but the bow only hurt his hands. He gave up and passed the bow to the next man.

One by one, the suitors struggled to string the bow, but no one could. At last only two suitors were left: young Eurymachus (yoo-RIM-uh-kus) and the mighty Antinous. Eurymachus struggled greatly, but he could not bend the bow. Angry, he handed the bow to Antinous.

Antinous laughed as he took Odysseus's bow in his hands. He placed one end of the string at the bottom of the bow and stretched the other end of the string toward the top. Inch by inch, the string moved closer. Antinous was panting now, his body straining with the effort.

Penelope stared in horror as the bow bent and the string brushed the top. Suddenly the bow flew out of Antinous's hands and clattered on the ground.

A loud laugh broke the silence. "What kind of man is this who cannot string a bow?" taunted a voice from the corner. Everyone turned in surprise as Odysseus, still disguised as the old, ragged beggar, stepped forward.

Antinous laughed scornfully at the beggar. "I'm tired of having you here," he sneered. "Whoever you are, you are no longer welcome!" He kicked the beggar's legs out from under him, sending the old man tumbling to the ground.

"Stop it!" cried Penelope as she hurried to help the stranger to his feet. "He is a guest in the house of Odysseus, and he shall be treated properly."

The beggar let Penelope help him up, but he made sure that he did not look directly at her. It took great restraint not to tell Penelope who he was. "I see there is a contest for the hand of this beautiful queen," he said. "I would like to enter it."

"Impossible!" Antinous roared. "You are nothing but a poor beggar."

"The contest is for anyone," Penelope argued. "If this man would like to enter it, then he shall."

"That's right," Telemachus said. "Mother, I

ask you to go to your room now. It is time for me to command what is done with this bow."

Penelope was astonished to hear her son speak this way, yet she did as he asked. Once she was in her room, the goddess Athena put a sleeping spell on her so that she would not hear the violent battle that was to come.

As soon as his mother was safely upstairs, Telemachus handed the bow to the beggar. The stranger stepped into the center of the room. With one angry look at Antinous, he bent the bow and easily attached the string. The crowd was frozen with surprise.

Without a pause, the beggar fitted an arrow into the bow and aimed it at the row of axe-heads. Then he drew the string as tight as it would go and let the arrow fly. WHOOSH!

Streaking like a bolt of lightning, straight and true, the arrow sailed cleanly through the twelve small holes and pierced the wood of the pillar on the other side.

The crowd exploded into chaos. Then something happened that was even more amazing. A golden light glowed around the beggar, then faded into nothingness. There stood Odysseus, his eyes ablaze and his iron muscles rippling along his mighty frame. King Odysseus, the rightful lord and master of Ithaca had returned.

15
The Final Triumph

Hey, guys. The man is back. Let's see what happens to Odysseus and Telemachus. Get ready for a terrific battle!

A wave of panic swept through Antinous as he saw Odysseus standing there. "Get him!" he shouted at the other suitors. "Kill him!"

The suitors ran for their weapons, only to discover they were gone. Telemachus and Eumaeus had hidden them well.

Odysseus drew an arrow from the quiver and fitted it into the bow. Then he fired at Antinous.

The arrow struck the suitor squarely in the neck. Antinous gagged and fell to the ground—dead.

Eurymachus rushed at Odysseus, but the mighty king was too quick for him. Another arrow found its mark, and Eurymachus too fell dead on the floor.

The suitors grabbed anything that could be used as a weapon while Odysseus stood as steady as a rock and let loose his deadly missiles. Suitor after suitor fell victim to his arrows, until at last the arrows were gone.

Then Telemachus retrieved the swords he had hidden by the door and joined his father at the center of the room. But one of the suitors had discovered where Telemachus had hidden the other weapons. The suitors hurried to arm themselves.

Athena, goddess of wisdom, did not forget Odysseus. She fought with him, protecting him and giving him supernatural strength. Telemachus fought bravely at his father's side, as strong and skillful as his father.

"You fight well, my son!" Odysseus shouted

as Telemachus's sword found another victim.

"Thank you, Father," Telemachus said, pleased at the compliment. "I want to be as mighty a warrior as you."

"You are," Odysseus said proudly.

Finally the fighting was done. Only Telemachus and Odysseus were left standing. All the suitors had either died or run away.

Odysseus called for Eurycleia, the elderly nurse who had recognized him from the scar on his foot. "Good woman, go and tell Penelope I am here, and that I wish to see her," Odysseus told her.

Eurycleia hurried upstairs to tell the queen the wonderful news. "My lady, your husband is home, and he has rid the house of the suitors," the old woman said.

Penelope did not believe her. "Don't mock me, Eurycleia," she scolded her.

"I am not mocking you. Odysseus is really downstairs, and he wants to see you."

Penelope leaped to her feet with joy. She could hardly move as thoughts raced through her mind. Could it really be her dear husband? She held her hand to her mouth as though in shock. She stood for several moments without breathing, and it was as if time and everything around her ceased to exist. Then she began to breathe and her heart began to beat wildly. She ran down the stairs, nervous and excited to see her husband after so many years.

The king and queen stood in the middle of the great hall. Neither of them knew what to say. They stood in silence, staring at each other as if they could never look long enough. Finally they ran into each other's arms. Penelope held her husband close and vowed that she would never let him leave again.

Brave Odysseus, the mighty king of Ithaca, was home at last.

What a great ending! The suitors are gone, Odysseus is home, and he is reunited with his wife.